TANYA LANDMAN

100%

Illustrated by Judy Brown

A & C Black • London

For Tilly

Chapter One
An Australian Boar

'Yuck! It's got horrid piggy eyes!'

Piggy eyes? Piggy eyes?! Of course I've got piggy eyes. What does she expect? I'm a pig! I'd look mighty strange without them.

That's the problem with living on a rare breeds farm: putting up with the people that come on the weekend can be really hard. Pig ignorant, most of them. It's not that I mind the occasional visitor, you understand. Not so long as they show a little respect for my pedigree.

I'm a pure Tamworth, me. That's the oldest breed of pig there is. Call me an old boar, but I can trace my ancestors right back to the Stone Age. I'm practically porcine royalty. My family started off as Brits, but then my Great-Great-Great-Great-Great-Great-Great-Great-Great-Grandad emigrated to Australia about a hundred years ago.

I got sent back to England when I was no more than a small piglet. I'm here to enrich the breed's bloodline, whatever that means. Still got my accent, though. Kept my Aussie twang. The point is, I come from ancient stock. I'm your actual living history. I'm quality, me.

Which was more than could be said for the little madam who was dangling her legs over the wall of my sty.

'It's ugly, Daddy! Daddy! It smells!'

Hurf! Everyone's allowed to break a little wind now and then. It's only natural. 'Specially if you've just had dinner.

'Daddy, that smelly pig's the wrong colour!'

Now I get it, I thought. I'd met her type before. She was one of the 'Babe Brigade'. They expect all pigs to be bright pink, with a stupid dinky wig, and never grow up. They showed us that film on the plane over, and that pig never got any bigger. All year long he was the size of a cutesy little piglet. He had a real serious growth problem. Hurf! Didn't anyone call the vet? What's more, I know for a fact that that pig dyed his eyelashes. I mean what kind of behaviour is that for a self-respecting porker?

But it's what some visitors expect. They peer over the wall and then jump back in shock when they see me – 600 lbs of ginger Tamworth boar. Got the looks of a film star, I have. I tell you, I'm a glorious sight to behold. 100% pure pig. That's me.

But madam on the wall just looked at me sniffily. It was starting to irritate me. So I thought, OK I'll go back inside. Burrow under my straw and wait 'til she goes away.

'Daddy! It's going away! Tell it not to! Bring it back, Daddy!'

And can you believe it? Daddy fetched a stick. That's right. A stick. And he started banging the back of my shed. Well, that just about did it for me. I was enraged. 100% furious. And an enraged, 100% furious, pure Tamworth pig is not a pretty sight, believe me.

Now I might be big, but I can sure run fast when I've a mind to. I came out of that shed like an oiled cannonball. I was headed straight for madam. She scrambled backwards off the wall with a really satisfying shriek. One of her shoes fell off in the rush. It landed in my trough.

I didn't even stop to sniff it.

Chomp. Gulp. Down in one.

Well, I am a pig, aren't I? We'll eat anything. It's what we do. It's our mission in life: Total Omnivorousness. Now there's a good word. Meaning 'can and will eat everything'.

But now madam was gasping and screaming, 'It ate my shoe, Daddy! Daddy! Get it back! Get it back!'

Daddy and me took a good long look at each other. I bared my teeth in a porcine grin. Dared him to try – just try – retrieving it. Daddy went pale.

'I'll get you some new ones, darling.' There was a distinct tremble in his voice. Daddy led madam away across the yard.

I stood up on my back legs and hooked my trotters over the sty door. 'That'll teach you to mess with a Tamworth, mate!' I yelled after them. 'Don't come back.'

I don't reckon he knew exactly what I was saying. There aren't many people that understand pig, 'specially when it's spoken with an Aussie accent. But they got the gist OK – they rushed back to their car real quick. And I lay down in my straw to enjoy the sunshine.

Chapter Two
Bellyaching

My nap didn't last long.

I guess shoes aren't all that digestible. After about half an hour my gut started to ache. By teatime I was feeling really miserable. I was breaking so much wind that even I was finding the smell a bit strong.

But only a dead pig doesn't get hungry. I swung my front legs over the door, and demanded my tea.

'Oy, Waiter!' I squealed, 'Where's my tucker?'

The Waiter came out of the farmhouse, grumbling to himself, same as usual.

'Some days I wish I'd never gone into farming. Dishing out food morning, noon and night. Shovelling up muck the rest of the time. What a life!'

Round and round the yard he went.

'It's not like there's any money in it. Worst business in the world, this is.'

Grumble, grumble, grumble.

'Bank constantly on my back. Bills landing on the mat every morning. Some days I think I should just sell up and have done with it. Find an easy job instead. Maybe I could work in a nice warm shop.'

He was as slow as ever. I swear he did it to wind me up.

First he went to all the cute fluffies. The itsy bitsy bunnies and the springy little lambs. Then he did the woollybacks and the bendyhorns. I mean they're in a field for heaven's sake. Food constantly all around them. They don't know the meaning of the word hunger. Then he did each and every one of my wives, and all my offspring.

By the time he got to me I was fair bellowing in desperation. 'About time! I'm starving!'

But before he tipped in my tucker, the cheeky beggar sniffed the air.

'Ooooh, Terence,' he said. 'You don't smell too good. Have you got an upset stomach? Perhaps we ought to give your insides a rest. Maybe you should miss a meal…'

I nearly fainted. Miss a meal? Me? I started to grunt and make pathetic little wheezes.

'Go on, mate,' I gasped. 'Tip it in my trough.'

Believe me, a 100% pure pig being reduced to begging for food is not a pretty sight.

Luckily Tamsin came across the yard just before I sank to my knees and pleaded. I mean it wouldn't have been dignified – a pig with my pedigree. But she spared me that humiliation.

She's all right, is Tamsin. She's the Waiter's daughter and she hands out the grub some days. When it's Tamsin's turn I can rest assured I'll get my tucker first. She leaves the fluffies and the woollybacks and the bendyhorns and all my wives and offspring until last. She's my Chief Back Scratcher too.

'Can't you see he's hungry?' said Tamsin. 'Come on, Dad. Give poor Terence his tea.'

Like I said, she's all right.

But then the Waiter started going on about the dreadful smell. You try eating a shoe, mate, I thought. See what it does to your insides.

Tamsin was great. 'He's desperate, Dad. I'm sure he'll be OK. Anyway, you can't bring his food all the way over and then take it away again. It's cruel.'

The Waiter gave one of those almighty, all-right-have-it-your-own-way-but-I-know-I'm-right sighs.

He tipped the tucker in my trough. It was only pig nuts, but it tasted like best swill to me. I pigged it in seconds. Pure heaven.

I felt all right for a minute. But then everything started exploding inside. 100% pure bellyache. My guts felt like they were being squeezed by a giant fist. Real nasty.

And as if that wasn't bad enough, then I got another shock.

'Going to help me bring Jolene over?' the Waiter said to Tamsin.

'Sure,' she replied.

Well excuse me. No one asked if I wanted company. Talk about lack of respect.

Jolene's one of my wives. A quality boar like me gets to have a lot of wives, see? I had six at the last count, just like Henry VIII. Told you I'm practically porcine royalty. They're nice enough girls, most of them. Apart from Jolene. Of all the sties in all the farms in all the world, I sure didn't want Jolene in mine. But they steered her over anyway – she practically galloped across the yard – then they locked her in. Hurf!

Jolene's lousy company. The worst. Never stops talking. And it's never about anything interesting – like my pedigree. It's always farmyard stuff. Beryl did this and Sheila did that, and who's had the biggest litter. And that night, when I had fireworks going off in my belly, she was the very last pig I wanted to see.

For starters I can't understand a word she's saying. She talks through her snout. Got a real thick accent.

'Hallo, Terrrence ow are yow?'

And she started doing this weird thing with her eyelashes: batting them up and down. I thought maybe two flies had simultaneously dive-bombed into both her eyeballs.

'You OK?' I asked.

'Oh, oim foin thenk yow, Terrrence. Thenks for arsking.'

And she did it again. Blink, blink, blink. Flutter, flutter, flutter. Then she came over and stood real close. Leant against me like I'm a gatepost or something. Talk about being over-friendly.

'Well this is exciting iddn't it?' she said. 'We heven't sin each uther in evver so long. I bin feelin evver so lonely, now me little piggies hev flown the nest.'

Pigs flying? I thought. What is the old sow on about?

'It's evver so noice to sae yow, Terrence.'

Blink, blink, blink. Flutter, flutter, flutter. I couldn't bear it. I went in my shed and buried myself under the straw without saying a word. I tried to go to sleep. I would have done too, if Tamsin and the Waiter had shut up for long enough.

'He's definitely off colour,' said the Waiter.

'Maybe he's just tired,' said Tamsin.

Too right, Tamsin. Good on yer, mate.

'No... He really ought to be showing some interest in Jolene. Something's not right. We're going to have to call the vet out.'

Wonderful. Fantastic. Marvellous. Well, I thought, that *really* gives me something to look forward to.

Chapter Three
The End of the Road

You've probably heard the expression, 'squealing like a stuck pig'? If you value your ear drums it's a noise best avoided.

Someone should have warned the vet. You'd think it would be part of his training. He didn't even bring ear plugs.

The second that man came into the sty, I knew he was trouble. His boots were too clean for starters. I could practically see my face in them. They were shiny. New. Untested. Just like him.

'This your first job?' asked the Waiter.

'Oh gosh, yes. I've only just qualified.' The vet smiled nervously. 'I'm afraid I'm a little inexperienced with … larger animals.'

Now if the Waiter had had any respect for me at all he'd have sent the fella packing. Called in a proper vet. But did he? Hurf!

'Oh, I see what you mean about the smell. It's not quite right, is it? Hmmmm.'

Can't a pig break wind without the whole world commenting on it? Where's my privacy?

If Tamsin wasn't at school she'd have seen me right. But that Waiter treats me like an *animal*.

'Better take a look at him, I suppose.' The vet's voice was kind of high and squeaky. He was real scared.

'He won't do anything,' said the Waiter. 'He's quite the gentleman, our Terence. He's a placid old thing, really.'

Oh yeah? I thought. Sounded like a challenge to me. I stared at the vet. Just you try any funny business, mate. I'll show you 'placid'.

The vet poked and prodded and peered into my little piggy eyes. He gave my belly a good hard squeeze. Then he said, 'He does seem a little off colour. I'll give him a shot. See if that perks him up.'

Just the sound of it perked me up all right. I can't stand jabs.

The Waiter got out of the way pretty sharpish. 'I'll leave you to it,' he said. 'I'm sure you can cope. I'll just go and … do … something … over … there.'

I was backing away into a corner, but the vet was coming for me. He had a whopping great needle in his hand.

'Come on, old chap,' he was saying. 'Easy does it. There's a good piggie.'

I charged. Did the old oiled-cannonball routine. Sent the fella flying. He was clever though. I gotta admit that. As he soared through the air, he made a lunge for my back. Stuck the syringe between my shoulders before he hit the ground.

That was when I started squealing.

The vet lay there like a dead man until I stopped. It was quite a time. I mean it took me ages to shake the needle out. In the end, I scraped it off against the wall of my sty.

When everything was quiet, the Waiter came back. He looked over at the vet lying there in the muck. I'd done a real good job on his boots. Couldn't see anything in them now. He was starting to look like a proper vet.

'Are you OK?' said the Waiter.

'Pardon?' said the vet.

'Are you OK?' the Waiter said, a bit louder.

'Sorry … can't quite seem to … pardon?' The vet was tapping the side of his head like he had water in his ears. I'd stunned his eardrums, see? He couldn't hear a thing.

'ARE YOU OK?'

'Oh, about six months ago,' said the vet.

'What?' said the Waiter.

'Yes, half-past two.'

The Waiter gave up trying to talk. He helped the vet up and let him out of my sty.

'That should perk him up soon,' said the vet. 'But if it doesn't… Well, he is getting on, isn't he? If he's not showing any interest in the sow, it might just be his age. Maybe he's reached the end of the road.'

What was he on about? What road? I haven't been anywhere! Doesn't anyone talk any sense around here? I was thinking that maybe the vet had done his head in when I knocked him over.

But then the Waiter started nodding. 'Well I have been thinking about it,' he said slowly. He sounded real sad. 'Perhaps you're right… Maybe it's time I brought in a new boar.'

'Pardon?' said the vet.

• • •

Well a new boar didn't sound too bad to me. We could have a few drinks, share some swill, swap a few stories, compare the length of our pedigrees. Yeah, I thought, maybe I'll get some good company for a change.

But when Tamsin came home she went ballistic. I could hear her shouting at the Waiter all the way across the yard.

'You can't do that to Terence!'

She was well and truly upset.

'Tamsin this is a *farm*. A rare breeds farm. We have to face facts. He's past it,' said the Waiter.

Passed what? I thought.

'But it's Terence!' she pleaded. 'He's special!'

She's a great girl, is Tamsin.

'I know, love. And I know you're fond of him. I am too.' The Waiter's voice went all funny and choky for a minute. 'But there's only one thing we can do when animals don't earn their keep. You know that, Tamsin.'

'But…!'

'No, love. I'm sorry. Things are rocky enough with the bank. We're only just keeping afloat as it is. We don't keep pets. We can't afford it.'

What's he on about? I thought. Floating round rocky banks? I reckoned the Waiter had gone soft in the head.

• • •

Tamsin came out later, after I'd had my tucker. Her eyes were all pink and puffed up. They looked a bit like mine. She scratched my back for ages, but it was like her mind wasn't really on it. She kept missing the really itchy bit, no matter how often I told her where it was. It was real strange because she's usually good at understanding pig, despite my accent.

Sometimes her eyes were leaking: she kept dripping on me and making me damp. Then she said, in a voice that was all husky and broken, 'Oh, Terence. I'm really going to miss you.'

I didn't like the sound of that at all.

Chapter Four
Betrayed

It was an act of low-down cunning. I was shocked. I didn't think the Waiter was capable of such evil. I mean I knew he was a bit dodgy. I've seen what he can do to a chicken when it's stopped laying, and believe me, it's not a pretty sight. But I didn't think he'd stoop that low. Any further down and he'd be in the sewer.

I'd never have set foot in that lorry if I'd had my wits about me. But he drove me mad, see? He never brought me my breakfast.

I mean have you ever heard of such an act of criminal cruelty? Can you imagine what it does to a pig of my size? The man should be reported.

I was hanging over my gate squealing for my tucker. I watched him do the rounds of the fluffies and the woollybacks and the bendyhorns and all my wives and offspring. When he got to me, all he did was scratch my ears and say, 'Later, Terence. You'll have to wait.'

Wait? Wait?! Me???

I started screaming for the RSPCA. But by the time Tamsin was ready for school I'd gone quiet.

I was on my knees, desperate for food. My head was swimming. My legs had gone all limp. Even my bristles had started to sag. I was starving, for heaven's sake. Fading away before my piggy eyes.

Tamsin came over. She was still all pink and puffy. 'Oh, Terence,' she said in this weird little choky voice. 'You know, don't you? You know!' Then she started leaking again, and dripping all over me.

25

And I was thinking that they'd both gone completely bonkers when the Waiter drove a lorry into the yard.

I'd seen it before. It was one of those ones with the slatted wooden sides and a long ramp. I'd watched the Waiter load up woollybacks and bendyhorns and drive off. There was something peculiar about that lorry, though, because they never came back. Not one of them. That lorry always came back empty. It's not that they were mates, or anything, but even so. You can't help wondering how they disappeared.

The Waiter lowered the ramp. He opened the two wooden gates that went across the back. It was pretty dark in there. Real nasty. Never in a million years would you get an intelligent animal like me to go up that ramp, I thought.

But then that low-down-despicable-evil-cunning devil of a Waiter brought out a bucket of swill. I could smell it all the way across the yard. It had all my favourite things in it too. Baked beans and boiled potatoes and stewed apples and whole bananas in their skins and slices of toast and thick lumpy custard. And even in my weakened condition, I managed to haul my front end over the sty door.

My grunt had gone all faint and pathetic. 'Tucker … tucker … please…'

I said 'please'. Can you believe it? A pig of my

pedigree reduced to that. Like I said, the Waiter should be prosecuted.

I can hardly bear to think about what he did next. It was barbaric.

He wafted the bucket under my snout. Let me drink in the smell of warm swill.

Then he took it away.

I went mad. Stark-staring-raving bonkers. I was out of my mind. Squealing and screaming and swearing. You've never heard such dreadful language. Tamsin put her fingers in her ears. But do you know what? The Waiter was wearing ear plugs. *Ear plugs.* You know what that means? It was a premeditated act of cruelty. He'd *planned* it. That's a hanging offence in my book.

He put the bucket down right where I could still see it. I never noticed 'til later that it was in the lorry. All I could see was food. FOOD! I was desperate!

The Waiter stood by the ramp. Then he shouted to Tamsin, 'Let him out!'

And Tamsin, with a face like a thousand sorrows, gasped an agonised 'sorry!' and opened my gate.

600 lbs of pure Tamworth has never moved so fast.

I was across the yard and into the bucket like a giant ginger bullet.

It was only when I'd finished my tucker – in about three seconds flat – that I realised I'd made a seriously big mistake.

Chapter Five
Trapped

The Waiter closed the gates on me before I'd finished my food. I didn't know he could move that fast. It was quite a surprise.

Tamsin came across the yard and peered into the back of the lorry. Her eyes were leaking so much that I thought she might shrivel up any minute – like a raisin, or one of those sun-dried tomatoes.

Then she looked at the Waiter. A great soulful silent plea for mercy. He didn't even glance at her. Couldn't meet her eyes, the low-down, deceitful scumbag. He went off and rummaged around in the cab of the lorry.

Tamsin and me were left alone. She didn't say a word. Just heaved and sobbed with these sorrowful little burbles. Tragic, it was. Tragic. Poor girl was setting me off, too. I was doing these pitiful, huffling grunts of sympathy. We were in a right old state. I didn't know what to do with myself. It was horrible in there. And I was thinking, Why doesn't she just open the gates so I can get back to my sty?

But then suddenly Tamsin stopped leaking. She stared at the metal hinges that fixed the gate onto the lorry. She went all tense and stiff, like she'd been jabbed with one of those electric cattle prods. There was a new expression glimmering in her puffy eyes – a flicker of hope.

A door slammed at the front of the lorry. The Waiter was coming back.

Quick as a flash, Tamsin reached down and pulled something out of the hinge at the bottom. It looked like a piece of metal to me – a wire peg or something. (The Waiter's always been a bit sloppy with his workmanship. Mends things with bailer twine and bits of wire. Like I said, the man's dodgy.) Then Tamsin gave me this real significant look – eyebrows raised, head cocked to one side. It was like she was trying to tell me something.

I squinted at her through my little piggy eyes. For the life of me I couldn't figure out what she was on about.

The Waiter was acting real shifty. Couldn't look at her, couldn't look at me. He moved Tamsin carefully out of the way. Took her by the shoulders and steered her to where the school bus was waiting. When she was gone, he raised the ramp.

I was shut in the dark.

• • •

I didn't like that journey. Not one little bit. I still had bellyache for a start. That shoe had given me the trots. I tell you it's real hard to keep your footing going round corners when you've covered the floor in runny dung. It went on for ages. We were going miles and miles and miles away from home. Every minute took me further away from Tamsin and my nice warm sty.

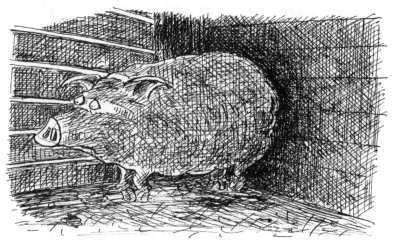

After about an hour, I could smell something in the air. Not my dung – this was something else. Something that was getting stronger and stronger every second. Closer and closer. Something that was making me real scared.

Fear. I could smell fear on the air. Not just fear. It was total, mad, crazy horror. Somewhere, close by, a bunch of animals were petrified.

And there I was, shut up in the dark.

I started with a few troubled grunts. As the smell got stronger, I changed to a nervous squeal. Soon I was screaming in terror.

Then the lorry stopped.

I could see through the slatted sides. The Waiter had parked in a yard. It was a bit like the one at home. There were pens of animals. But there was this weird kind of path, too, with great bars either side. It trundled along all on its own, into this huge great barn. And that's where the smell was coming from.

I stayed right at the back of the lorry. I wasn't moving for anybody. A load of woollybacks did, though. Another lorry was parked next to us. A man lowered the ramp and opened the gates at the back and off they went. Straight out of their lorry and up that path. Right into the building, meek as lambs.

They didn't come out.

And I knew then that if I let them get me on that moving path – if they got me into that building – I wouldn't come out either. Not ever.

When the Waiter lowered the ramp and opened the gates, I was just plain terrified. At least he had the decency to look miserable. His eyes had gone all pink and puffy, just like Tamsin's.

The Waiter had parked the lorry so I'd go straight down the ramp and onto the path.

But I wasn't shifting.

So this great big burly fella with one of those cattle prods in his hand came into the lorry and made straight for me. He had an evil grin on his face. Looked real mean.

My mind went completely blank. I wasn't thinking about escaping. I wasn't thinking full stop. My head was bursting with pure white terror.

Then the man slipped.

I never thought I'd be grateful to madam's shoe for giving me the trots. But when he skated across the floor of the lorry and crashed into the side (jabbing himself in the backside with his own cattle prod on the way), my mind suddenly cleared.

And that's when I made my bid for freedom.

Chapter Six
Running Wild

There was no way I was running down that ramp. So I started rooting around for another way out of the lorry. I was hurling myself against the gates, slamming into them, and blow me down, one of them shifted. Just a bit. It lifted up in one corner exactly where Tamsin had taken out the wire. I reckon that's what she'd been trying to tell me. Clever girl. She'd fixed a way out. Like I said, Tamsin's all right.

By now the man with the prod was getting up. He was swearing something terrible. Looked real angry.

I drove my full weight against the gap. Rammed into it. 600 lbs of pure pig smacking into a wooden gate with only one hinge. It didn't stand a chance. Trouble was there was nothing between the gate and the ground but a load of empty air. So this particular pig flew for a whole metre before slamming into the tarmac head first.

It wasn't nice. Not one bit. I bruised my snout real bad. Thought I was going to end up looking like one of those weird Vietnamese pot-bellied porkers.

But worrying about losing my film-star looks was the last thing on my mind. The prod man was coming for me, and this time he had help.

'Pig's out! Pig's out! PIG'S OUT!' The shout echoed round and round the yard. And all of a sudden there were dozens of them – big, mean-looking fellas with blood-stained clothes – coming out of that building. They had me surrounded.

I was scared. But I was angry too. Enraged. 100% irate. With a squeal of pure fury I ran at the man nearest me. I managed to get my head between his legs and with a great jerk of my snout I threw him aside. He screamed nearly as loudly as me. That struck terror into the rest of them. They started to run in all directions. Couldn't get out of my way fast enough. I went completely berserk, crashing into animal pens, smashing fences, trampling anyone stupid enough to get in my path. Problem was, I couldn't see a way out of the yard. I was going round and round in circles. Getting more and more demented.

That's when I spotted him. The Waiter. Standing by a gate. It was the way out. And the gate was still open.

Prod man was yelling, 'Shut the gate! Shut the gate! SHUT THE GATE!'

And the Waiter did shut the gate. Or at least he started to. But I tell you something peculiar – he was mighty slow about it. I mean, I know he can move real quick when he wants to – I've seen him shift. But he was walking slowly, sort of fumbling with the catches. It was like he wasn't trying. And when I pelted past him, I got a glimpse of his face – I could have sworn the Waiter looked pleased.

Chapter Seven
Town Centre

I charged down that road. Didn't have a clue where I was headed. I just wanted to get away from that place. That smell of blood and fear. I wanted it right behind me. I kept running. Running and running and running, until my trotters were sore and my legs had started to ache.

There I was. Belting along a twisting country lane. Totally lost. Totally terrified. Miles and miles from home. It was real scary stuff.

Plus it was all a big shock to my system. I mean, I'm more of a short-sprint-across-the-sty kind of a pig. I'm not so hot on the long-distance stuff. I wasn't built for running marathons. Eventually I just had to slow down. A terrible, screaming stitch in my side was stabbing away at my ribs – hurt worse than my aching belly, it did.

There was a nice muddy puddle at the side of the lane, so I flopped down into it for a bit of a wallow. I'd just started to get my breath back, when I heard this faint trip-trapping noise from somewhere behind me. It was round the corner. The hedge was too high for me to see what was making it, but it sounded a bit like footsteps. Someone was trying to sneak up on me. I jumped out of that puddle real fast. I was off.

I wasn't paying any attention to where I was going. I was lost anyway, so it didn't seem to matter much. It wasn't until the hedges stopped and the houses started that I began to get worried. It was slow at first – a bungalow here, a little row of cottages there, a couple of fields in between. The next thing I knew there were houses on both sides of the road and I was completely hemmed in. It was like a maze. Buildings everywhere. And no matter how hard I tried to find my way out, I just seemed to get further and further in.

I ended up on this long, straight road. The buildings on both sides had huge windows stuffed with all kinds of weird things. It was real busy, too. There were cars everywhere – their brakes squealing like stuck pigs when they saw me: 600 lbs of pure Tamworth in the middle of the road.

There was a whole bunch of people on the pavements, pointing and staring. They were excited, I guess. Well, it's not every day practically porcine royalty trots down the street. A little boy in a pushchair was totally awestruck. 'Big pig!' he gasped. 'Look at the great big pig!'

I liked the sound of that 'great'. He was a cute kid. Had the right attitude. But I couldn't stop and make polite conversation. I had to keep going. I mean, I was terrified that Prod man was going to show up any second. And every now and then I got a snatch of that trip-trapping noise from somewhere behind me.

I was almost out of there – finally I could see beyond the buildings to where open fields began – when I came to this big, black, flat place, full of hundreds of cars just sitting there, motionless. It was weird. Like they were waiting for something. And right in the middle was this huge, square building. It was massive.

There was a whole line of these funny-looking wire baskets on wheels perched outside the entrance. People were flowing in and out of that building like a bunch of ants. And the glorious smell of food was wafting out – fresh bread and cakes and chips and peas and baked beans. I was drawn towards it like a magnet. I mean, a pig's got to eat even if he is on the run. And I was half-starved after all that exercise. I was desperate for some tucker.

I galloped up to the glass doors, wondering how on earth I was going to get in there. But those doors just whooshed open like magic as soon as my snout pressed up against them – it was like they were expecting me.

Chapter Eight
Pig Heaven

As soon as I got in there I knew I was in Pig Heaven. Right in front of me there was a whole load of bananas – piles and piles of them heaped up – just lying there looking ripe and luscious. They were begging to be eaten. And beyond that there were mountains of apples and heaps of oranges and stacks of pineapples. It seemed to go on for ever. There were potatoes too, and they're one of my favourite things. OK, so they were raw – I mean I'm usually more of a boiled potato kind of a pig – but that day I wasn't feeling too fussy. I reckon I'd have eaten anything. I started on the bananas. I was so starved I hardly even bothered to chew the skins.

Suddenly there were people all over the place. There was a whole load of screaming and shouting and millions of flapping arms. You'd have thought they'd never seen a pig before. I carried on eating, but it wasn't long before there was this horrible screeching wail, and a car with a blue flashing light pulled up outside those glass doors.

The next thing, there's this man in a blue suit and a funny-looking hat giving me a long, hard stare. He started advancing on me with a stick in his hand and fear in his eyes.

'Steady on,' he said, nervously. 'There's a good pig. Let's get you out of here, nice and safe.'

Well, after my experience with Prod man, I wasn't taking any chances.

I made a break for those doors, but they weren't whooshing any more. Blue-Suit man must have fixed them shut, sneaky devil.

I was trapped. But I sure wasn't going to go quietly. I shot past the fruit and veg. People were leaping out of my way left, right and centre. Trouble was, I couldn't see where to go. I reckoned there had to be another way out somewhere, so I was bombing around. I'd never seen so much food in one place. Galloping past without eating any of it was torture. And I'll tell you something else, those shelves were about as well built as something the Waiter had made – things kept falling over. Every time I turned a corner there was yet another crash. Shockingly bad workmanship, it was. Dreadful.

When I got into the far corner of the building, I stopped in my tracks. I'd pelted down the whole length of it, and suddenly, there in front of me was a whole load of freshly baked bread. It was all lined up, side by side – crusty … brown … irresistible. Not just bread, either. There were cakes and sticky pastries and gooey biscuits. My mouth was watering so much I thought I was going to drown in my own saliva. I had to eat some of it. I had to. Show me a pig who could have gone past that lot without stopping and I'll show you a dead porker. Down it went – I managed a couple of loaves and a dozen sticky buns before Blue-Suit caught up with me.

That's when I spotted the way out.

Behind all the bread and cakes and stuff there was this vast kitchen. Massive great ovens; sack-loads of flour; trays and trays of eggs; barrels of syrup; boxes of icing sugar. No wonder it all smelt so good.

It was hotter than the Australian outback in that kitchen, but from somewhere wafted a cooling breeze. Right at the very far end there was a door. An open door. A door to the outside. A door to freedom.

You've probably heard the expression 'A Bull in a China Shop'? Well, believe me, a Bull in a China Shop's got nothing on a Pig in a Kitchen. The mess was spectacular.

I shot through that place faster than you could say 'Impressive Pedigree'. Course the mess wouldn't have been quite so bad if the people in there had got out of my way fast enough, but they were real slow movers. The guy with the eggs just stood there, eyes popping, mouth hanging open. Blocking my escape route he was, and I wasn't stopping for anything, not with Blue-Suit on my tail. So I did my oiled-cannonball routine – sent the fella flying. He soared through the air.

Splat! Splat! Splat! Eggs rained all down my back. Terrible waste of good tucker, it was. Shocking.

After that they all started climbing onto work surfaces, hiding under tables. They were dropping stuff all over the floor.

I was nearly at the door – I could smell the scent of freedom – when I skidded in a puddle of melted butter. Lost my footing totally.

600 lbs of Tamworth boar slammed sideways into a set of shelves. They didn't stand a chance. It was amazing. Like some sort of freaky storm.

Clang! A vat of golden syrup burst right open. Oozed across the floor in a sweet, sticky flood. *Phtt! Phtt! Phtt! Phtt! Phtt!* Raisins pelted down like little black hailstones. *Pwoof!* Icing sugar and flour billowed out in huge clouds. Blue-Suit couldn't see me for dust. Literally.

I finally emerged into the sunshine looking more like a Large White than a ginger Tamworth. But I didn't have time to worry about spoiling my movie-star complexion. I sped away as fast as my legs could carry me. Pretty soon I was back in the countryside, pelting up a twisty little lane.

Eventually the hedges stopped. I'd reached a stretch of open moorland, so I got off the road and onto the grass, which was much easier on my poor sore trotters. When I got far enough away I stopped for a rest. I found another nice big muddy puddle to have a wallow in, and I was sitting there quite happily, elbow-deep in water, when I heard that trip-trapping noise again, and this time it was real close.

That's when I realised that I'd been followed.

Chapter Nine
Fugitives

There were five of them.

Three woollybacks.

One stinky old billy goat.

And the weirdest-looking chicken I'd ever seen.

She was massive – taller than the Waiter, I reckon, with this spookily long neck and bald legs. Bet she lays big eggs, I thought. Wouldn't mind one of those for my breakfast.

When I'd escaped from my lorry, and was crashing around in that yard I'd smashed through a few pens, see? I'd let all that lot out by mistake. They were covered in flour from Pig Heaven. It was amazing. They'd followed me the whole way. And now the woollybacks were looking at me with big adoring eyes, like I was a hero.

But company was the very last thing I needed. I mean, I was a fugitive. I needed to lie low. Stay out of sight. Move under cover of darkness. I couldn't do that with a six-foot chicken following me.

So I said, 'Scram!'

They just stared at me. All of them. Without saying anything.

'Go away!' I said.

They didn't budge, so I heaved myself out of my wallow and turned and walked a few steps. They followed, like a bunch of blooming sheep.

I said, 'GO AWAY! CLEAR OFF! SCARPER!'

But then one of the woollybacks took a step forward. She cleared her throat and said – real polite – 'Actually, sir, if it's all the same to you, we'd rather stay with you. Please, sir.'

And the other two bleated, 'Please, sir! Please, sir!' Like we were in a cave and they were the echo.

And I thought, If it's all the same to me? If it's all the same to me? Of course it's not all the same to me! On the other hand, I rather liked the sound of that 'sir'. Showed proper respect, if you know what I mean. I'd had precious little of that lately.

It was like the woollyback sensed I was softening up a bit.

'We're just sheep, you see, sir. We're not clever animals. Not like yourself, sir. Oh the brilliance, the cunning, the sheer audacity of your escape!'

I didn't know what 'audacity' meant, but I got the general picture. I mean, I could tell from her expression that she was bowled over by my bravery. There was no stopping her.

'Your kind heartedness, your generosity in freeing such ignorant beasts as ourselves. Oh, sir, we'll follow you to the ends of the earth if you'll let us.'

'Let us!'

'Let us!'

You know, I always thought woollybacks were stupid, but these three seemed like bright girls. I thought to myself, well OK, maybe I could use a little company. But I'm not sure about him.

I took a good long look at the billy goat. He was chomping on an old plastic bag that he'd pulled out of the grass. He stared back with those horrible slitty goaty eyes. I mean their pupils go the wrong way – side to side instead of up and down. It gives them a real mad, bad look. Once he'd swallowed the bag, he hoiked and spat on the grass.

Hurf! People say pigs have got no manners. They've never met a billy goat is all I can say. I mean they are disgusting! And in the breeding season … phew! They smell foul. Rank. Like sweaty cheese. Sour milk. Rancid butter. Real nasty. And they never stop widdling. Drip, drip, drip. Like a leaky water trough. He was doing it then – while he found an empty crisp packet and started to eat it. He was gross.

But before I got a chance to say anything, the chicken went bonkers.

'P... P... P... P...' She couldn't seem to get the words out. She was flapping her wings and waggling her head from side to side. That's the problem with chickens. Small heads. No room for a proper brain in there.

'P... P... P... P...'

We were all staring at her, thinking she was going to have a seizure. Maybe the excitement had been too much for her, that the poor girl was going to drop dead there and then.

But she finally got the word out.

'P... P... P... P... PEOPLE!'

She was right. There was a line of people stretching across the horizon. The Waiter was there. Mr Blue-Suit. And Prod man. Plus a few others from that horrible building with their blood-stained aprons. And – which was really weird – there were a couple of people with cameras. (I'd had enough visitors pointing cameras up my snout back at the farm to know what *they* were.)

All we could do was run.

Chapter Ten
Leader of the Pack

That chicken could shift, I'll say that for her. She was over the hill before the rest of us were half-way up. Then the stupid bird came back. Like I said, there wasn't much of a brain in there. She didn't like being out ahead on her own, but she couldn't slow herself down either, she was in such a flap. So she just kept running round us in great big circles. So much for lying low. We couldn't have stood out more if we'd tried.

Still, by the time we got to the top of the hill, the people were quite a way behind. Two legs just don't go as quick as four. (Not unless you're a giant chicken.) So I had time to get a bit of a look at the countryside. In the distance – not too far away – was a nice big patch of woodland. No one was going to be able to catch us there. Even if they followed us in, it would be dead easy to give them the slip. It was the perfect hiding place.

And that was where we ran, as fast as our legs could carry us.

We stopped running as soon as we got into the trees. There was too much undergrowth to go flat out, but we were well hidden so I wasn't too bothered about going fast any more. We had to keep stopping for the chicken in any case. She was so tall she kept banging her head on branches. And every time she did, the thing kept shrieking, 'P... P... P... PANIC!'

She was getting herself in a right old flutter. Poor bird was a complete nervous wreck.

There was a big, grassy clearing right in the middle of the woods. We stopped for a rest and a bit of tucker. Grass for the woollybacks, bit of vegetation for the chicken, and an old wellington boot for Stinky Billy.

I had a good rootle around and came up with all sorts of stuff. I had bits of plant and bugs and slugs and a few fat worms. It was OK. In fact it was quite nice for a while. Made a change. But then I started dreaming about buckets of warm baked beans and custard, followed by a good thorough back scratch from Tamsin. And as it started to get dark, I had a pang of homesickness so bad I had to sit down.

It was just as well the woollybacks were there. Molly, Holly and Dolly, their names were. They kept my mind off things. They were real good company. Bright girls. Dead interested in my pedigree.

We sat in that clearing like cowboys round a camp fire. (Only we didn't have a camp fire, obviously. I'm not *that* clever.) Even the chicken managed to sit down and relax for a bit.

I told them about all my ancestors, starting with my Great-Great-Great-Great-Great-Great-Great-Great-Great-Grandad. Now *he* was a pig of character. He led the family emigration to Australia. We were needed out there, see, on account of us not getting sunburnt like those wimpy dinky-pinky Babe types. He was a real outback pig. A rough tough rugged porker pioneer.

I filled those girls in on all my relatives, all the way back to the Stone Age. It took a little while, but they kept nodding, and bleating, 'Maa, maaa, maaarvellous.' So I knew they were real fascinated.

Of course Stinky Billy kept spitting every time I got to a good bit. It was like he wasn't interested in my family history. Can you believe any creature could be so uncultured? I mean, I'm aristocracy, me. Plus I'm the hero that saved his life. And all I got from him were those slitty-eyed looks and a smattering of spit every now and then. Hurf! That creature is a waste of space.

By the time the moon came up everyone was flat out and fast asleep in that clearing. Everyone but me. I lay there and looked up at the stars feeling real sorry for myself. Because I knew that whatever happened next, I was never, *ever* going to be able to go back to my nice warm sty.

Chapter Eleven
Wild and Free

That living-in-the-wild business isn't nearly as great as it sounds, believe me. It wasn't a patch on my home comforts. It was cold, it was wet, and I had to rootle around all day to get enough tucker. From sunrise to sunset it was dig, dig, dig. Exhausting. My snout got real sore after the first day.

Of course it wouldn't have been so bad if we could have got out of the wood. After that first night in the clearing, we tried to move on to pastures new. I led the woollybacks and the chicken down to the edge of the wood. Stinky Billy followed along behind, snatching at old scraps of paper and plastic.

But when I poked my head out from behind a bush there were a load of blinding flashes, and the deafening clicks of cameras. It was worse than a bank holiday at the farm.

'Back, girls!' I shouted. 'Get back!'

We all retreated to the safety of the clearing.

'OK,' I said. 'Looks like we'll have to stay here then. I guess we can manage…'

The woollybacks nodded. They were real happy to have a quality pig in charge. Stinky Billy just stood staring at me all slitty-eyed, saying nothing. He was eating a long piece of material – it looked like he'd managed to rip the end off someone's coat before we'd bolted back to the clearing.

I started to grub around for my breakfast, but I've got to admit I was worried. Something mighty strange was going on. I'd got a bit of a look at those people outside the wood. There was a whole bunch of new ones who were smart looking, with shiny, unused boots and clean white raincoats – just like the vet. They had flashy cars too – cars that weren't used to being driven across muddy fields. And it wasn't as if they were trying to round us up. They never even tried to come in. They were just out there. Surrounding the wood. Watching. Waiting. It was weird.

• • •

Later that morning, the Waiter tried to catch me. At least, I think that's what he was up to. He walked into the woods rattling a bucket of pig nuts. I reckon he thought I might follow him out like a dog. Well I'm an intelligent animal, me. I wasn't going to walk into the trap. Not this time. Not now I knew what he was capable of. I sneaked after him through the undergrowth.

I thought I could ambush him – knock him down and swallow the pig nuts real quick. But before I had a chance to carry out my plan, he emptied the whole lot out, gave me a huge wink and walked away. It was like he wasn't trying.

He did exactly the same the next day. And the next. And the next. Four mornings on the trot he crashed around in the undergrowth and then emptied out a load of pig nuts. And one afternoon I was rootling around in the bushes when I heard the Waiter talking to the Shiny-Boot Brigade outside the wood. Going on about how fond he was of me, and how he'd only done what he did because he didn't have any choice. I didn't have a clue what was going on.

● ● ●

Like I said, it wasn't comfortable in that wood and by day four the place was starting to look more like a battlefield than a woodland. The woollybacks and the chicken had eaten every single blade of grass. Stinky Billy had cleared out every ounce of rubbish. He'd started on the vegetation in sheer desperation. Stripped it bare of everything reachable. And me – I'd turned over every square inch of earth looking for food. Seemed there wasn't a single worm, bug or beetle left in the whole wood.

On the fifth morning, the Waiter sneaked into the clearing at the crack of dawn. Frightened the life out of me, he did. I mean it wasn't even light. Everyone else was fast asleep, but I woke up to find the Waiter sitting there on a tree stump right next to me. I leapt to my feet, prepared to run for my life, but all he did was tip a huge bucket of swill on the ground.

Then he sat there, talking to me while I scoffed the lot.

It wasn't his usual grumble, grumble, grumble either. Something funny was going on, because the Waiter sounded cheerful.

'They love you, Terence!' he said. 'It's astonishing. They're all desperate for your story. You could get us all out of deep water. If you carry on like this, you'll get the bank off my back. Who knows? We might even end up rolling in it! That would be nice, wouldn't it, old chap?'

Didn't the Waiter ever talk sense? I mean, as far as I could see there wasn't anything on his back, let alone a bank. And there sure wasn't any deep water in sight. As for rolling in it... Rolling in what? I thought. I'm not rolling in anything with you, mate. Not after what you did.

After I'd finished my swill, he said, 'Better get back, I suppose. Don't want anyone to see me, do I? Don't want the press to suspect that I'm aiding and abetting you...' He made this strange noise at the back of his throat. I'd never heard him do that before and it gave me quite a shock – the Waiter was *laughing* – he was chuckling to himself.

Then he stood up and gave me a bit of a scratch between my shoulder blades. It had been so long since anyone scratched me that I shut my eyes and heaved a deep sigh. It was heaven.

Before he left he said, 'Just another day or so, that's all. Then I'll keep you in clover for the rest of your days. That's a promise, old son.'

Clover? Clover?! Who wants to be in clover? Like I said, he never talks any sense.

• • •

Later on that day, I was grubbing around in the bushes desperately looking for bugs, when I heard some of the Shiny-Boot Brigade talking to each other.

'Farmer can't seem to lure his pig back, can he?' one said.

'No...' said another. 'I hear the owner of the wood is getting impatient.'

'Yes,' said the first one. 'I gather he's got plans to flush them all out.'

I didn't like the sound of that at all.

Chapter Twelve
Mud Bath

On day six we woke up and realised we were completely out of tucker. It was desperate. I was going mad with hunger. My belly was rumbling and aching something terrible. I was ravenous.

We sat there in what had been the clearing, and which was now a muddy mess. Stinky Billy had chewed the tail feathers off the chicken during the night. Her rear end looked really tasty. Now I don't usually go for uncooked tucker. I'm more of a warm beans and custard sort of a pig. But like I say, I was desperate. I licked my lips. But then the chicken stood up and I had a good look at those long bald legs of hers. Mighty powerful kick, she had. Tackling her would be real tricky...

So I looked at the woollybacks. They were smaller than me. Defenceless. My mouth started to water. They must have noticed the hungry gleam in my eye because they kind of huddled together nervously, and then Molly said, 'With all due respect, sir...'

'Respect, sir…'

'Respect, sir…' echoed Holly and Dolly.

That brought me back to my senses. Respect. What was I thinking of? I mean these girls were depending on me. I was the leader of the pack. I had responsibilities. I gave my head a shake and tried to listen.

'We wondered if maybe … possibly … well, you know best of course, sir… But we wondered if we ought to think about moving on…'

'Moving on…'

'Moving on…'

'Exactly,' I said decisively. 'That was exactly my plan… Clever of you to guess, girls. Well done.'

Molly, Holly and Dolly were all attention. (So was the chicken, but I didn't look at her. I was trying hard to ignore that appetising rump steak.) I ignored Stinky Billy too, for obvious reasons. That creature hadn't said a single word the whole time we'd been trapped in the wood. Just spat and widdled and chewed endlessly. He was getting on my nerves.

'Right, girls,' I said. 'We're going to have to break out of here. We'll wait until it's dark. And then … then we'll run for it.'

The girls were all nodding eagerly, 'Yes, sir.'

'Yes, sir.'

'Yes, sir.'

But Stinky Billy burped loudly (like I said, that creature has no manners), then spat (disgusting!) and said, 'That's it, is it? Your plan?'

Well being as those were the first words he'd bothered with in five days, you'd think he'd have come up with something a little more helpful. He had one of those toffy British accents that are really irritating.

He spat again, 'Is that the best you can do? A pig of your pedigree?'

That got right up my snout. I walked up to him, looked him in the horrible slitty eyes, and growled, 'Have you got a better idea?'

He spat again. (Where did it all come from? How could any animal have so much liquid in it?)

'Might have,' he said.

'Oh yeah?'

'Yes.'

'Yeah?'

'Yes!'

'Yeah?'

'YES!'

'Well, what is it then?' I demanded.

That stopped him. For a minute, at any rate. He lifted a hoof and scratched his ear, considering. Then he hoiked and spat on the ground.

'When I was regimental mascot for the 17th Royal Fusiliers...' he began.

'You were in the army?'

'Yes indeed.'

I noticed the woollybacks looking at Stinky Billy. They had started to do that weird thing with their eyes – just like Jolene. Blink, blink, blink. Flutter, flutter, flutter.

Stinky Billy didn't react. 'My old sergeant major was a great believer in diversionary tactics,' he continued.

'Oh yeah?'

What on earth are 'diversionary tactics'? I thought.

'What we require,' said Stinky Billy, 'is for one of us to create an enormous disturbance on one side of the wood, while the rest of us slip quietly away out of the other side.'

'Well done, mate,' I said. 'You're right. That was exactly my plan. I was just getting round to explaining that bit when you interrupted.' (Well, I would have thought of it, if he hadn't insulted my pedigree. He got me all edgy.)

'Now,' I said firmly, taking control. I mean, I was leader of the pack, not him. 'We just have to decide who's going to create the diver... diver... diver... you know ... noise and stuff.'

'I would have though that was obvious,' said Stinky Billy.

'Oh yeah?'

'Indeed. The task should fall to the one amongst us who is most noticeable.'

We all turned and stared at the chicken.

Chapter Thirteen
Diversionary Tactics

There was one big problem: that bird's brain was tiny. Trying to get her to understand my plan was real hard. And there was no way she was going to go down to the edge of the wood on her own. When I tried to persuade her, she went bananas – flapping her wings and swinging her head from side to side.

'P... P... P... P... Petrified!' she squawked. She was getting herself in a right old state.

'Perhaps the bird requires support,' said Stinky Billy.

'P... P... P... P... Please?' The chicken looked at me with these big, pleading eyes.

'Support...' I said slowly. 'Yeah... OK...' I didn't know what he meant. The chicken looked sturdy enough to me.

'Maybe we should split up,' Stinky Billy carried on. 'Hoofed animals one way, smaller-brained animals the other.'

I knew he was talking about the chicken, but even so, it was really irritating. And the woollybacks were doing that blink, blink, flutter,

flutter thing at Stinky Billy. Well, I sure wasn't going to let him lead them anywhere. Not without me – that creature wasn't to be trusted.

'No,' I said firmly. 'We're a pack. We stick together.'

The woollybacks looked at the ground.

I cleared my throat. 'I think it's time we all remembered who set us free in the first place, don't you?'

That did the trick. The girls looked real sheepish.

'Yes, sir!'

'Yes, sir!'

'Yes, sir!' they bleated, meek as lambs.

Like I said, they were bright girls. Respectful of my pedigree. Not like some.

'Ah well…' Stinky Billy sighed. 'I concede there might be strength in numbers…'

I didn't have a clue what 'concede' meant, but I knew I'd won the argument. Quite right, too.

So in the end we all went down to the edge of the wood with the chicken. She didn't want to be seperated from the rest of us until the very last moment. I reckoned we could all hide in what was left of the bushes while the chicken did her stuff. Once she was safely away we could double back through the wood and make a break for it.

'Look,' I said to the chicken for the millionth

time as we squelched through the muddy remains of the undergrowth. 'All you've got to do is go out there and flap around a bit. Get them to follow you, see? Lead them away. Then you can outrun them and catch up with us later, OK?'

The chicken looked at me with her big, scared eyes. Poor bird was beside herself. But she went out into the open anyway, brave girl, and as soon as she'd set foot out there she went totally bonkers. I could hear her flapping around all over the place. She was doing a real thorough job of attracting attention. I couldn't resist having a quick look to see if my plan was working. But when I stuck my head out, I got the shock of my life.

The Shiny-Boot Brigade had vanished.

There was just one muddy truck, two mean-looking men and this strange, scary, yowling noise. Made my bristles stand on end, it did.

The chicken's neck was swaying like she was caught in a force ten gale. 'P... P... P... P...' she started. It was like she was trying to tell me something. 'P... P... P... P...' But she couldn't get the words out. 'P... P... P... P...' she went on and on. 'P... P... P... P...' And at last she screeched, 'P... P... P... P... PUPPIES!'

I thought the old bird had really lost it this time. Dropped each and every one of her marbles.

But then those men opened the back of the truck. There was a whole bunch of them. And my last horrified thought was, they sure aren't puppies! Then I was running for my life.

They'd sent in the dogs.

• • •

You can imagine the effect a pack of slavering hounds had on the chicken. First of all she stuck her head down a rabbit hole. Tried to hide. Then, when one of them brushed past her, she fainted clean away. Slumped into a giant, mangled, feathery heap.

Me and the girls just ran for it. I guess Stinky Billy followed too. Judging by the smell, he must have been there somewhere.

I didn't know where we were headed. We just had to get away.

Away from those teeth. Those slashing, ripping, tearing teeth.

We ran right through the wood. Fled for our lives. Terrified. It didn't occur to me that those dogs were herding us – driving us ahead of them – into a trap.

We broke out of the other side of the wood real fast. And that's where all the Shiny-Boot Brigade were lurking – bunched together like a load of sheep. We ran straight into them.

Lights exploded left, right and centre. Cameras were going off all over the place. Something sharp hit me. Like a jab. But I couldn't see a vet close by. Once. Then again, twice more. I squealed like a stuck pig. And all of a sudden my legs went weak and wobbly and I fell over. Just like that. Crashed down on my side. Someone was waving a fluffy thing over my head. I wonder if that tastes good? I thought.

There was a clean pair of boots right next to my head, and a woman's voice was saying, 'We're coming live from the woods where Terence the Tamworth boar has just broken cover. Veterinary experts have darted him with tranquillisers. Here he lies, the pig of impeccable pedigree, who has captured the hearts and minds of animal lovers all over the world...'

'Impeccable pedigree… Impeccable pedigree…'
The words echoed round and round my head.
Then everything went black.

Chapter Fourteen
An Australian Star

When I woke up, I was lying on a bed of soft clean straw in my very own sty. Tamsin was scratching behind my ears. It was heaven. I thought for a minute I'd dreamt the whole thing. That none of it had happened.

'Dad! Dad! He's coming round!' Tamsin was calling for the Waiter, and he appeared in no time at all. He came scurrying across that yard like his wellington boots had been oiled. What's more he was carrying not one, not even two, but *three* buckets of swill. He emptied them into my trough. All my favourite things. Baked beans and boiled potatoes and stewed apples and whole bananas in their skins and slices of toast. And one whole bucket of warm lumpy custard. He must have made it 'specially. The Waiter poured it all over everything else. Marvellous. (You know, you can forgive someone a lot if they give you a whole bucket of custard.) It was heaven. Pure heaven.

After I'd finished it, Tamsin scratched my back. She listened properly to where the itchy bits were – 'left a bit, down a bit, across a bit.' And while she scratched, Tamsin told me the whole story.

I'm a celebrity. Somebody had filmed me trotting down the street in that town. And my little gallop through Pig Heaven had been caught on the security cameras. So my great escape made it onto the local news. I'd been on television. After that, seems everyone got interested – every news channel in the entire world, plus the newspapers. They all sent reporters to stand outside the wood. I was even on Blue Peter. I mean, how much more famous can you get? All those news people treated me like I was a hero – a porcine Robin Hood, or something – outwitting my enemies, evading capture, rescuing defenceless creatures from certain death. Which is all true, of course. So now I'm not only practically porcine royalty, I'm your genuine megastar too. The Waiter's even made a new sign for my sty. I knew I wasn't born with film-star looks for nothing.

Tamsin says I won't have to get on that lorry again. Not ever. The Waiter made a whole pile of money from selling my story. And you can't do away with a celebrity pig, can you? I can stay here. I'm a bona fide Number One Tourist Attraction, me. All the crowds and crowds of admiring visitors who want to see me now have to pay for the privilege. The Waiter's put up a new shed by the farm gate so he can relieve my fans of their cash. (Course, it wobbles a bit, but I guess it'll do the job.) It should keep me in baked beans and custard for ever. And the visitors will show a proper respect for my pedigree, now that I'm famous.

What's more the woollybacks and the chicken are allowed to stay too. They've got their own field right next to my sty. Molly, Holly and Dolly can hear about my family history every single day, lucky girls. They haven't said much – still speechless, I guess – but I reckon they're real delighted.

The Waiter's even made room for Stinky Billy. Hurf! Well I guess I can put up with him for a while. We're a pack, see? They called us 'The Birmingham Six'.

Once Tamsin had finished scratching, I lay down in my straw to enjoy the sunshine.

100% happy.

100% pig.

About the Author

Tanya Landman was born in Gravesend, Kent, and now lives near the sea in North Devon with her husband and two children. Before she became a writer, she had many different jobs. At one time Tanya worked in a bookshop, where she was allowed to read all the books before she sold them, and so developed a passion for children's literature.

Later on, she worked in a zoo and because she has always loved animals was very happy to cuddle red-kneed spiders and tickle hissing cockroaches. She also discovered that Brazilian tapirs go cross-eyed and roll over with happiness if you scratch them between the shoulder blades – just like pigs.

As well as writing books, Tanya also works with the Storybox Theatre company in Bristol.

About 100% Pig, Tanya Landman writes:

In 1998, two Tamworth pigs escaped from a sausage factory. They made the news headlines and became famous all over the world.

I thought the idea of a pig on the run was a great starting point for a book. I'd kept a pet pig for years – a lovely Vietnamese Pot Bellied sow called Tilly – so I knew a fair bit about how they behave and think: Porcine Perceptions!

I was thinking about the character of a pig, and started to wonder how a Tamworth might sound – what his voice might be like...

One night Terence – a custard-swilling boar with a fine Australian accent – rootled his way into my dreams and started talking about his impeccable pedigree. *100% Pig* is the result.

Another fantastic Black Cat…

PHILIP WOODERSON
Arf and the Happy Campers

Arf is older and (a little) wiser and
ready to embark on his first hilarious
full-length adventure!

Arf expects to have to stay at home
during the school holidays while his
sisters enjoy a trip to France. However, the
plans go awry and he finds himself running
a camping ground and re-enacting
a battle between the Saxons
and the Normans!

Another fantastic Black Cat…

SUE PURKISS
Spook School

What could be worse for a ghost than
not being spooky enough? That's
Spooker's problem as he faced his
all-important Practical Haunting exam.
It doesn't help that his task is to haunt
a brand-new house – hardly the kind
of dark, dingy place where ghosts
are meant to dwell!

But when Spooker makes a new friend,
he might just find a solution to
his problems…

Black Cats – collect them all!